BAKER AND TAYLOR

and the Mystery of the Library Cats

by Candy Rodó

PAW PRINTS PUBLISHING
pawprintspublishing.com

Book and Cover Design by Maureen O'Connor
Edited by Bobbie Bensur and Alison A. Curtin

English Paperback ISBN: 978-1-22318-377-0
English Hardcover ISBN: 978-1-22318-376-3
English eBook ISBN: 978-1-22318-378-7

Published by Paw Prints Publishing
PawPrintsPublishing.com

There's a library just like yours where two cat buddies – Baker and Taylor –spend most of their days, just lounging and reading, lounging and reading by the big, bright window.

These cats love books. More than they enjoy anything else. More than chasing mice. More than eating tuna! Baker enjoys reading about history and faraway places.

The stories Taylor enjoys always involve adventure.

Baker and Taylor are very different. Baker is serious and quiet. He reads to learn. Taylor is silly and outgoing. He reads for fun. But they are best friends, all the same.

One day, the librarian's cat, Flora, asks them, "Why are you two always here? You should get out more!"
"But I like it in the library," says Baker.

"Oh, you silly cat! There are other libraries!" suggests Flora. "You know? She's right!" adds Taylor. "We could go somewhere else! How fun!"

"If I were you, I'd go visit the New York Public Library! There are two cat buddies there just like you and Taylor," says Flora.

When they arrive at Pennsylvania Station, Baker and Taylor hop off the train, wearing backpacks filled with their must-haves. A guidebook for Baker and a sardine sandwich for Taylor.

"The guidebook said the quickest way to get to the main library is the subway," says Baker.

FROM BAKER'S GUIDEBOOK

Over 650,000 people travel through Pennsylvania Station (often called Penn Station) daily. That's even more than all of the people catching flights at New York City's three airports every day!

FROM BAKER'S GUIDEBOOK

New York City is home to over 8 million people, who speak more than 800 different languages. Welcome! ¡Bienvenidos! Bienvenue! Huān yíng!

When they reach the street, the cats are stunned.
So much to look at!

"Which way to the library?" Taylor asks a bodega cat nearby.

"Keep going that way," says the bodega cat. "Down 42nd street. You'll see it!"

As they walk, the cats try to look up! But it's hard to see the skyscrapers. All they see are legs. Big legs. Short legs. Legs in pants. Legs and tiny socks. Legs of all colors.

All they hear are loud noises. Cars honking. Cell phones ringing. Pushcart vendors laughing loud. A little voice saying, "Let's go see the library cats!"

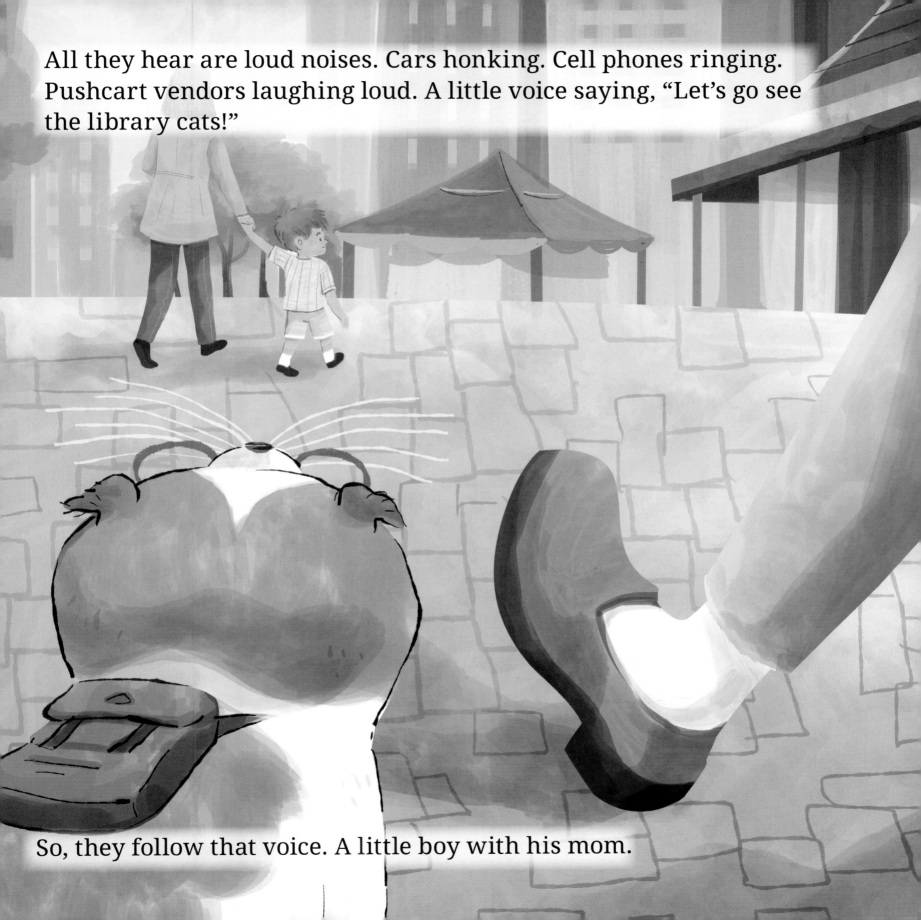

So, they follow that voice. A little boy with his mom.

Soon, Baker and Taylor find themselves in a beautiful park. But they don't see any library cats.

GERTRUDE STEIN

"Wait. Where's that little boy and his mom? We're lost! Let's ask this lady for help," suggests Taylor.

"That's no lady. That's a statue!" says Baker.

"A library is a library is a library," the statue of Gertrude Stein tells them.

They ask another statue, Mr. Goethe. "Do you know where the library cats are?"

"I despair to tell you, I do not know of these cats you ask about!" he tells them.

GOETHE

FROM BAKER'S GUIDEBOOK

There are nine monuments in Bryant Park, including sculptures of famous writers and politicians, like Gertrude Stein, Johann Wolfgang von Goethe, Benito Juárez, and William Cullen Bryant, among others.

"Well, they weren't helpful," says Baker.
"Nope. But, what do they know? They never go anywhere!" answers Taylor.
So, they decide to go back to 42nd street, just like the bodega cat told them.

Finally, they see a banner. "New York Public Library!"
"That's it! Let's find those cats and introduce ourselves," suggests Taylor.

The library is beautiful. And HUGE! Much, much bigger than their library. No cats in sight, though.

Suddenly, they hear, "Let's go see the library cats!"

Baker and Taylor are excited to follow the voice, but it's disappeared into the crowd.

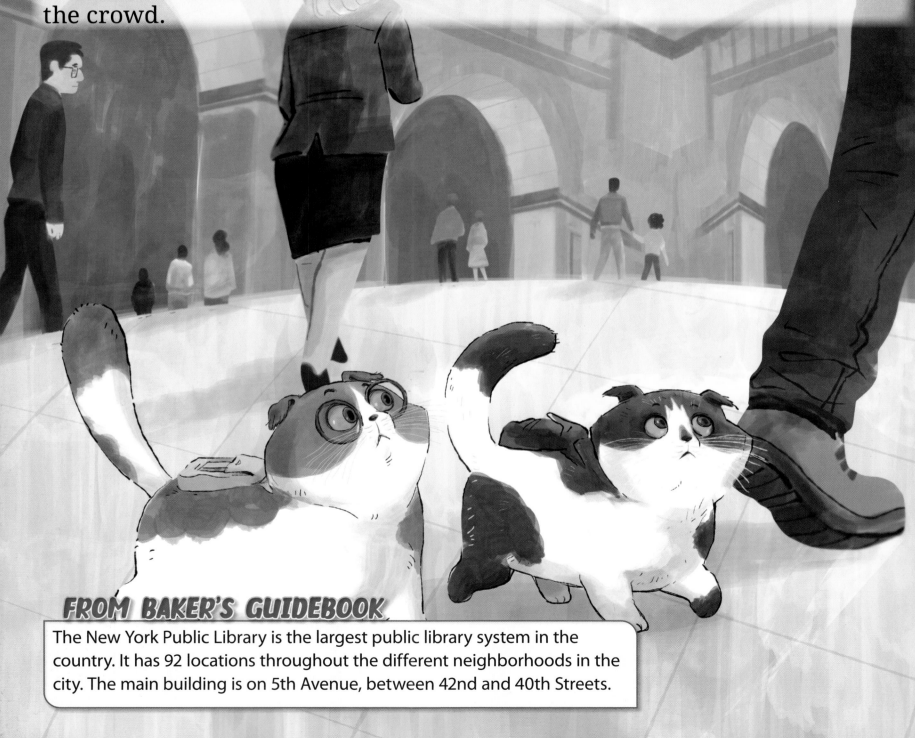

FROM BAKER'S GUIDEBOOK

The New York Public Library is the largest public library system in the country. It has 92 locations throughout the different neighborhoods in the city. The main building is on 5th Avenue, between 42nd and 40th Streets.

But, Baker and Taylor don't give up. Instead, they roam the halls, looking for the cats. Soon, they find themselves in a big room with many shelves of books.
"Maybe one of these will help," thinks Baker.

Taylor has other ideas.

"While you read, I'm going to go see if those cats are at the pizza parlor across the street."

"You just want to get a slice. With sardines, I bet," whispers Baker.

"Maybe," says Taylor.

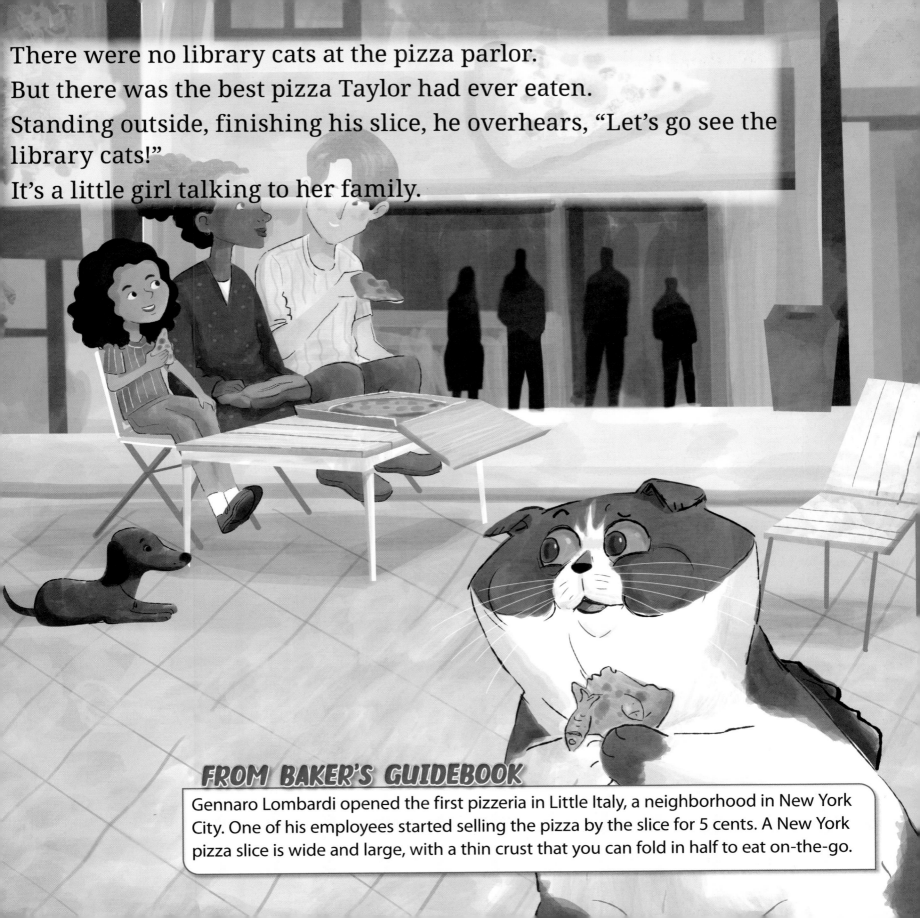

There were no library cats at the pizza parlor.
But there was the best pizza Taylor had ever eaten.
Standing outside, finishing his slice, he overhears, "Let's go see the library cats!"
It's a little girl talking to her family.

FROM BAKER'S GUIDEBOOK

Gennaro Lombardi opened the first pizzeria in Little Italy, a neighborhood in New York City. One of his employees started selling the pizza by the slice for 5 cents. A New York pizza slice is wide and large, with a thin crust that you can fold in half to eat on-the-go.

Before they can run off, Taylor scurries over to their dog. "Okay. I got to know! Where are these library cats?!"

"Library cats? You're looking at them!"

Taylor can't believe it. He runs to find Baker.
"I found them! I found the cats!" he screams.

"I found them," he whispers. "They are outside."
"Library cats *outside* the library?" asks Baker.
"Yes! Come, I'll show you!" insists Taylor.

"Here they are! Baker, meet Patience and Fortitude!" says Taylor. **Two lions. The library cats!**
"Nice to meet you!" the lions say.

"Oh, I understand now!"
says Baker. "Lions *are* cats.
A type of cat anyway."

"Yes! Hey! Let's take a selfie with our new friends."

FROM BAKER'S GUIDEBOOK

The two marble lion sculptures, *Patience* and *Fortitude*, have been guarding the main building of the New York Public Library since 1911.

And, as they do, Baker and Taylor decide they want to do more of this travel thing...

But, first, they're going to read a good book.

The New York Public Library

- The New York Public Library (NYPL) was founded in 1895. It is the largest public library system in the country. With 92 locations across the city, it provides free books, movies, information, and education services. All you need to access them is a library card.

- The main branch of the New York Public Library is located on 5th Avenue between 40th and 42nd Streets. The main building was opened in 1911. It was built on top of one of New York City's first public water systems, The Croton Aqueduct. When the aqueduct became outdated, the city decided it was the perfect place to build a new library–enough space for a large marble building and a public park behind it called Bryant Park. The site was already deep because of the water system that was first there, so the library now had plenty of basement space for bookshelves. The library has a basement of seven floors and over 80 miles of shelves.

- The sculptures of the lions outside the library, named Patience and Fortitude, are made of marble from Tennessee. Marble is a type of stone that is used to create many buildings and sculptures. It can withstand all types of weather over a long time. The New York City Mayor at the time of the Great Depression, Fiorello La Guardia, gave the lions their names. He felt New Yorkers most needed these two qualities to get through those tough years. Patience is the ability to stay calm during difficult situations and fortitude is the mental strength needed to face danger with courage.

- Besides housing millions of books, the NYPL has also been home to the original toys of Christopher Robin, Winnie-the-Pooh and his friends, Eeyore, Tigger, Piglet, and Kanga since 1987.

- Other non-book objects that can be found in the New York Public Library's main branch are Charlotte Brontë's writing desk (that still has a lock of her hair in one of the drawers), maps used by sea captains (and maybe even pirates!) dating back to the 1400s, the writer Jack Kerouac's harmonica, and the first printed edition of *The Star Spangled Banner*.

- Many blockbuster movies have been shot in the NYPL, including the original *Ghostbusters* and *Spider-Man*.

Sources: nypl.org; gothamist.com/news/underneath-the-new-york-public-library

Other landmarks of New York City

From Baker's Guidebook

- New York City runs on a public transit system, and trains are very important there. **Pennsylvania Station** (also called Penn Station) is the busiest train station in the Western Hemisphere. However, the largest train station in the world is located across town from Penn Station, and is called **Grand Central Terminal**. Grand Central covers 48 acres and has 44 train platforms, more than any other railroad station in the world. Its platforms are all below ground, going down three different levels. Grand Central has restaurants and offices for the NYC Transit Authority – the department that keeps subways, buses, and ferries running smoothly throughout the city. It even has two libraries and an indoor tennis court.

- The **Empire State Building** was built in 1931 and took just 401 days to complete. Over 3,500 workers helped build it, including expert iron workers and iron welders from the Mohawk Nation in Northern New York State. These workers call themselves "skywalkers" because they have worked on many famous skyscrapers in New York City. The Empire State Building was considered the tallest building in the world for 41 years, until the Twin Towers were built in 1973.

- Today, the tallest building in the city and in the entire Western Hemisphere is called **One World Trade Center** and can be found at the very southern tip of NYC. It opened in 2014 and rises 1,776 feet into the sky.

- One of the most iconic landmarks of New York City is the **Statue of Liberty**. This giant sculpture was a gift from the people of France. Lady Liberty has lived on Liberty Island, in the New York Harbor, since 1886.

- Smack dab in the middle of the city is **Central Park**. The park was created in 1858, and over time has changed a lot. You can find dozens of statues in Central Park – just like the statues that Baker and Taylor met near the library – of writers and musicians, animals, soldiers, and even a few famous storybook characters. There is a zoo, two ice skating rinks, playgrounds, baseball and soccer fields, and plenty of pretty walking paths to explore.

Sources: wtc.com/about/buildings/1-world-trade-center; wsj.com/articles/SB1000142412788732399860457856352042419529; grandcentralterminal.com/; centralparknyc.org/park-history